The
Little Brown Donkey

by

Kathleen C. Dahlquist

Kathleen C. Dahlquist

THE LITTLE BROWN DONKEY

Published by

FEATHER FABLES PUBLISHING COMPANY
The Pattison Building
260 W. Miami Avenue
Venice, Florida 34285

Library of Congress Catalog Card Number 94-71676
ISBN: 0-9634122-8-0

Dedication

I dedicate this book to my children, Dick, Edna, George, Diane, Sharon, Philip, and their families.

My thanks and appreciation to my dear friend, Victor L. Hubert and to the members of the Venice Writing Class for all their support and encouragement.

The Little Brown Donkey
Table of Contents

Chapter I

The Little Brown Donkey

"Oh dear, oh dear—how I wish I had a friend! It gets so lonely here by myself," said the little brown donkey. He stood, day after day, in a small pasture near a road where cars passed by. Once in a while a person would walk by. Or someone on a bicycle, but no one paid any attention to the sad little donkey.

Not far away in a field there was a herd of cattle grazing. There were brown cows, black cows, and a few red and white cows. They munched on the grass as they moved around their large pasture. The young cows, or calves, followed along, stopping their nibbling to play with each other. With the cattle there were many small white birds. Each bird seemed to stay close to one particular cow.

The little donkey watched, occasionally twitching his long ears to better hear the mooing sounds that the mother cows were making as they called their calves to their side.

"I wish I could moo," thought the donkey. "Maybe then the cows would talk to me too." He didn't think that he had better bray as donkeys do, because a bray is a loud, harsh sound. "If I try to say 'hello' I may frighten the cattle and they would run further away."

"It's just not fair," said the donkey, stamping his foot angrily. "No, it's just not fair. I have no one to stay by me. No one at all. The cows have each other and they have all the calves running around, playing happily, having lots of fun. And they have the white birds too. While here I am with no one to talk to, no one to nibble the grass at my side. Oh, dear!"

The little donkey let his head droop and his whole body seemed to sag as he shifted his weight from one foot to another. He certainly looked forlorn and unhappy. Just as he was breathing a big sigh, he felt something, or someone, brush his hind foot ever so gently. He turned his head to see what had touched him. And there, close by his hoof, was a small white bird. "I must be careful not to step on him," thought the donkey.

"Hello, little bird," said the donkey. "How nice of you to come visit with me. I've seen so many white birds like you walking in the next field. You each seem to have a special cow that you follow around. You just don't know how I've wished that one of you would come to see me."

"Thank you for such a warm welcome," replied the little white bird. "I've seen you here every day too, and I decided to see for myself if you would like a friend. Would you?"

The donkey could hardly answer, he was so

surprised. Surprised and delighted.

"Oh, please, please do stay," he finally said. "You just don't know how very much I've wished for a friend. It's super! Now, since we are friends, shouldn't we have a name to call each other?"

"What a good idea!" replied the little white bird. "I've never really had a name of my own. I am an egret, and all those other birds over there with the cows are egrets too. Do you have a name? And, are you a tiny horse? Or maybe a pony?"

The little brown donkey laughed. His first laugh for ever so long. "No, I'm not a horse, even a tiny one. Nor am I a pony. I am a donkey."

"A donkey," repeated the egret. "Well, I've never had a donkey for a friend before. I know that you and I will get along just great!"

"I can't call you *donkey*, you know. You are a special donkey—my special donkey—and I must have a name for you!"

"And I can't call you *egret* 'cause there are lots of egrets, but you are my special egret and my special friend."

So the little brown donkey with his head held high, and with the small white egret hopping about his foot, began to think of a name for each other.

Can you think of a name for each of them?

Chapter II

The Donkey and the Egret Find A Name

The little white egret studied his friend as he sought a suitable name for him.

"Let me see—my donkey is small, he is brown, he has long brown ears and a short, swishy tail. He used to seem so sad, but now he stands with his head held high. His eyes are brown and soft and friendly. Shall I call him 'Brownie'—or 'Tiny'—or maybe 'Pedro,' as I've heard other donkeys called? No, I want a name that tells everyone that he is my special friend. Ah, I know. I shall call him 'Pal,' for that is what he is—my pal. I hope that he will like that name."

The little brown donkey too, was pondering over a suitable name for the egret. "Let me see—he is not a very large bird—but neither is he very small. He has such white, white feathers with buff plumes on rump and crown, and long slender legs. I like how he cocks his head from side to side as he follows along in my footsteps. His eyes are bright

4

and seem to see everything. Shall I call him 'Whitey'—or 'Spindle Legs'—or? Oh dear, none of those names will do! I want a name that says he's my friend. Ah, I've got it! I'll call him 'Pal.' I do hope that he will like that name."

"I've a name for you," called the egret, just as the donkey said, "I've a name for you, my friend." They both wanted to be first to tell the other what name they had chosen.

"Pal!" they both exclaimed together.

"What did you say, little donkey?" asked the egret.

"No, what did *you* say?" demanded the donkey.

And again, they both said, "Pal."

Well, when they realized what had happened, they stood there in the field, shaking with laughter over the joke. After a while the donkey said, "Thank you for wanting to call me 'Pal.' But we can't both be 'Pal,' now can we?"

"No," the egret agreed, "that would not work. We shall have to think some more."

"Well," said the donkey, being quite practical, "let's keep 'Pal' for one of us. And let's call the other a name that means a pal, too." So they thought and thought.

Finally the donkey said, "How about 'Chum'? That means a friend, a pal, too!"

"Great," said the egret, "you thought of 'Chum,' so I'll be 'Chum,' and you'll be 'Pal,' okay?"

"Okay!" agreed the donkey. "They are both good names, and everyone will know that Chum and Pal are best friends from now on."

Chapter III

The Friends

Chum, the little white egret, and Pal, his friend, the little brown donkey, wandered about the small corral where Pal had spent so many lonely days, weeks and months all alone. He was not lonely now. He and Chum shared happy, comfortable days and slept side by side at night. They were always together.

Liking each other so much, they begun to think of ways that they could help each other. Pal scratched up the earth with his sharp hooves, turning over the earth so that Chum could find lots of juicy bugs to eat. He had seen the cows doing that for the egrets over in their pasture.

Chum hopped on Pal's back, enjoying a ride but, at the same time, making sure that insects didn't bite the little donkey. He had noticed that the donkey could not get rid of the pests, no matter how much he wiggled his long ears or how fast he swished his small tail. It did not reach far enough.

6

As the days passed, the egret realized how little of the world could be seen from that tiny pasture. So one day he decided to suggest to Pal that maybe it would be fun for both of them if he were to fly a little way off, exploring the area. "Then," he reasoned, "I could come back and share my adventures with Pal." They would both learn about what was going on.

At first Pal was reluctant to let Chum fly away from his side. It was so nice having him so close by. But, he thought about it and thought about it, and finally agreed.

"Yes, Chum. I do think you have a great idea. You could fly over the whole farm and tell me about what you have seen. You could see what that funny 'quack, quack, quack' noise is that I hear from over the hill. Or you could find whatever it is that says 'bow, wow, wow.' I have often been puzzled about these and many other sounds."

"Also," continued the donkey, "I know you must yearn to fly again. I don't want you to get tired of being with just me either. Yes, Chum, we'd both enjoy your trips. We'd have so much to talk about when you return. Let's do it!"

So it was agreed. Thus began the adventures of Pal and Chum.

We'll read about them another day.

Chapter IV

Chum Goes Exploring

Soon after Pal and Chum had decided to learn about their world together, early one beautiful spring day, Pal was dozing on his feet—very relaxed, one leg slightly bent—his usual way of sleeping. He seldom lay down. Throughout his sleep he heard a noise in the distance. He perked up his long donkey ears, turning them first this way and that, just as radar turns, picking up signals. There it was again. He looked down at Chum, just waking up.

"What is it, Pal? What do you hear?" Chum asked.

"Shh, listen! There. Did you hear that?" asked Pal.

Chum was way down low and the breezes did not waft sounds to him as they did to the taller Pal and to Pal's long ears.

"What does it sound like, Pal?" asked Chum.

"It sounds like the wind, sort of," replied Pal.

"It says, 'hisss,' and then a 'quack, quack, quack!'"

Chum jumped up on Pal's back so that he could hear better. He too heard the "hisss" followed by a frightened "quack, quack, quack!"

"Sounds as though it is just over that little hill in the next field, Pal. I remember seeing a pond there when I used to fly into the cow pasture. I'll just go take a look. I'll be right back." And up into the air he flew, spreading his strong wings to catch the air currents. It seemed so good to be flying again! He circled the field, dipping low over Pal to let him know that he'd soon be back.

Pal watched his friend go high in the breeze, his white wings flashing in the sunlight. For a moment or two he felt a little sad. "What if Chum liked being away so much he would decide not to come back?" he thought. But then he reminded himself that they had agreed to explore this way, with Chum using his wings and his bright eyes to unravel some of the mysteries about them. What fun it would be later on as Chum related his experiences. And, while he was waiting, Pal munched the grass and kicked up little stores of insects for a hungry Chum to enjoy when he returned.

At last he saw the flash of wings as Chum sailed over the fence and landed at his side.

"What was it, Chum, what did you see?"

"Oh, Pal, I wish you could see it! Or rather, see them," replied Chum. "Remember I told you that I thought there was a pond just over that hill? Well, there is a pond, not very large. In the center is a thing that shoots the water high in the air. It looks so pretty. And the sound of the water splash-

ing makes you feel cool."

"Was that the thing I heard?" asked the donkey. "And did it say 'hisss' or did it say 'quack, quack quack'?"

"No, Pal, the water only made a splashing noise," explained the egret. "But I did see what made the other noises. There were two swans—white like me—but much, much bigger. They had very long necks. One was on a nest of straw under some bushes at the edge of the pool. The other swan was strutting up and down on the bank, watching his mate on her nest where she is hatching some eggs. And every time that the ducks swam close to shore, the big swan would ruffle up his feathers, arch his neck, and half run and half fly at those ducks, hissing loudly as he flapped his wings. He looked so cross!"

"Go on, Chum, go on—then what happened?"

"You should have seen those ducks turn quickly and swim back to the other side! They were so frightened! And they kept saying 'quack, quack, quack' as they hurried away."

"Well done, little friend," said the donkey. "Now I do not have to wonder about those noises. I can just picture the pond, the fountain, the nesting swan and the ducks all scrambling to get away from the angry daddy swan. Thank you, Chum. And now you can rest and enjoy all the insects I have been digging up for you."

Until Chum and Pal find something else to explore, we'll leave them browsing contentedly in the small corral.

Chapter V

Chum and Pal Meet A Monkey

"Clickety-click, clickety-clack." It seemed to be getting louder and nearer.

"What is that noise?" asked Pal of his friend, the egret.

It was still dark out in the field. The sun had not risen yet. The moon and the stars seemed to have dimmed their lights as the new day began.

"Clickety-click, clickety-clack, clickety-click, clickety-clack." It seemed to be coming closer and closer. Then there was the sound of steam as wheels locked on the track that ran along the other side of the ranch. There was a long whistle, followed by a shudder as the train came to a stop.

"What is going on?" asked the egret. "I hear yelling, I hear chains clanking, and I hear the noise of what must be a big, big cat, or maybe more than one cat."

"I don't know what it is," replied the donkey. "I remember hearing it just about this time last year, too. But I didn't see it then, and I can't see it now. I wonder what is going on."

The field where the donkey and the egret spent their time together happened to be just outside of a town where a big circus had its winter quarters. There was a train track seldom used any more except when the circus trains came back from their summer tour to spend the winter months in a warm climate.

The donkey and the egret listened and listened. There were so many noises, but nothing to see from their corral.

"Well, Pal, I guess I had better go over and see if I can find out what this is all about. See you later," he called as he circled the field, dipped low over the donkey and then soared up over the bushes.

"Hurry back," called the donkey. "I'll be waiting to hear all about it!"

As the donkey began to munch his breakfast, wondering what exciting story the egret would tell on his return, he heard a sort of chirping noise close by. "Now what can that be?" he pondered as he stepped close to the fence from where the noise seemed to be located. "It can't be Chum, because Chum would fly right down here where I could see him."

Just then, a small brown creature with very long arms and a very long tail swung down from a tree and stood right in front of the donkey. He almost looked like a human being for his front paws were like hands. But he had a small head, was furry and was very agile and quick. It sounded

as though he were saying, "Tsk, tsk, tsk."

"Hello," said Pal. "Who are you and where did you come from?"

"Hello, little donkey," replied the furry creature. I know you are a donkey 'cause I ride one that looks just like you. I am a monkey from the circus. The children come to see me and they bring peanuts."

"Oh my," said the donkey. "My friend the egret has gone to see what all the noises were. Won't he be surprised when I have a story to tell him? He won't believe I have met a monkey!"

"They will soon find that I am not there in my cage," said the monkey, "and they'll come looking for me. I will just wait here and talk with you until they do come. Is that okay?"

"Of course you may stay," replied the donkey. "But I have no food for you, and you must want your breakfast."

"That's all right—I have some bananas that I hid up in the tree. I'll get them and I'll eat them while you eat your breakfast."

When the egret returned after watching the circus train being unloaded, he was greeted by both the donkey and the monkey. He was so surprised!

After they had all had their breakfast, as the sun grew warmer and warmer, they gathered under a little tree near the edge of the corral. And there the egret told of all the things he had seen, while the monkey nodded his head when he heard the things he knew so well being described.

"There were cages and cages of big cats, Pal. Some had black stripes, some had big manes and tufted tails, and some had spots. They all paced back and forth along the bars, looking for a place to get out, I guess."

"Oh, those were the tigers and lions and leopards," explained the monkey. He even knew the big cats, as the circus people called them, by name. And he described the tricks that the cats did—jumping through burning hoops, across other cats' backs and sitting on perches in the center ring.

"Golly," said the donkey. "I certainly would like to see that, but I'd be afraid one might come after me."

"You should have seen the huge, enormous, gigantic animals that were helping pull the carts. Why, they could pull eight or ten at a time!" exclaimed the egret. "Their legs looked like pillars, and they had ears much bigger than yours, Pal. Oh, their tails were so small, but they'd walk along holding the tail of the one in front of them with what looked like a big hose for a nose!"

"They are the elephants," explained the monkey. "And they are much too large to be put in a cage. So they are chained to a very strong ring sunk in the floor in the elephant house. That long nose is called a trunk. It is used for gathering food, for throwing water over their backs on a hot day and for lifting things, too."

"I saw strong men working so hard that they looked as though they could do most anything. And I saw people all painted up with white, white faces, big red noses and designs of all kinds. And such funny clothes!"

"The workers are called 'roust-a-bouts,'" said

the monkey. "The painted ones are the clowns. The roust-a-bouts set up the circus. The clowns make people laugh. I do tricks with the clowns."

When the sun was almost gone for the day and the little donkey had listened to all the exciting stories about the circus, a man came looking for the monkey. The monkey jumped into the man's arms, glad to be going back to the life he knew in the circus. He was well fed always, and he enjoyed hearing the people applaud when he did his tricks with the clowns. Once again, Pal and Chum settled down for the night to dream of all the stories they had heard that day.

Just before they went to sleep Pal murmured a "Thank you, Chum," and Chum replied, "You're welcome, Pal. And I liked your surpise for me. I certainly never thought you would be seeing some of the circus too!"

Chapter VI

The Fire!

"Look, Pal, look over there. Is that a rain cloud I see this beautiful sunny day?" asked Chum.

Pal looked to the east where Chum was pointing and, sure enough, he did see a big black cloud. But on breathing in air, he detected something different. The breeze was blowing the cloud towards the pasture, and it had an strong odor. It stung his throat and made him cough.

"That's not a cloud, Chum. That's smoke! And smoke means fire, you know." All animals fear fire more than anything else.

"Fire! We had better try to get away from here, Pal," urged the egret. "But how can we? I can fly away, but you will have to break down the fence."

Pal looked at the fence with its strong poles driven into the ground. He pushed against one pole but it would not budge. He ran from post to post,

16

but none of them could be knocked down—even by a strong little donkey. The wires between the posts had sharp barbs that would tear the donkey's skin.

The smoke was going higher in the air, and it was now making both the donkey and the egret have trouble breathing.

Across the field, the cows were all hurrying up the lane to the cow shed where they went each night to be milked. The egrets had all flown away to a place far on the other side of the fire where the wind blew the smoke away from them.

"Let's try the gate," called the egret, who did not want to leave his friend while he found safety for himself. "I see some rope holding it shut. Maybe my sharp bill will tear the rope and the gate will swing open."

So Chum pecked at the strong rope while Pal got ready to kick the gate open as soon as the rope was off. But the rope was too strong and the egret had to give up, while the sharp smoke made him cough.

Just when the friends thought that there was just no escape, they heard a loud "weee" and a big bell clanging. Around the corner came a big shiny red fire engine. There were six men, all dressed in bright yellow slickers, big rubber boots and odd shaped helmets which covered the back of their necks. The engine had ladders, hoses, buckets, axes and all the other fire equipment needed for extinguishing fires.

The firemen saw the donkey and the egret, but didn't have time to stop. But they called to them and said, "Don't be afraid. We'll put that fire out very quickly." and off they went.

Pretty soon the sound of water being pumped out of that fire engine and onto the fire could be heard. The water sort of hissed as it hit the hot roof of the house that was burning.

In a short time the smoke blew away as the firemen squelched the fire. Once again the air was fresh and sweet.

"Wow!" said the donkey, "I'm so glad someone called the fire department. We couldn't have inhaled that smoke much longer, could we?"

"You are right," said Chum. "But I think we shall have you practice jumping so that in case of danger you could hurdle the fence and get away."

"What a good idea, Chum! Imagine me, a stubby little donkey, soaring over a fence as those beautiful jumpers do over there in the riding stable! We'll start right now."

And, as it grew dark, the little donkey trotted around and around in his corral, the egret mounted on his back urging him on, trying over and over to clear his hooves as he jumped over his bucket of drinking water.

Perhaps when we return we shall see Pal a steeple chaser and Chum a champion rider.

Chapter VII

Trouble!

The day started off as most of the days did. The sun seemed to come up as big and fiery red as it had been when it dipped below the horizon the night before.

The little brown donkey and his friend, the egret, woke up hungry for their breakfast. They began to follow along the fence, looking for some choice grass for the donkey. Often the grass outside the fence grew longer and greener than the grass inside the corral. So the donkey would lean over the fence to nibble what he could reach. He didn't forget to disturb the ground with his sharp hooves so Chum, the egret, could catch all the insects his hooves stirred up.

They hadn't gone too far when the egret said, "Pal, you are not turning up much for me this morning. And I'm very hungry."

"Sorry, Chum," answered Pal. "I didn't realize that you were not finding enough. I'll try to dig my

19

hooves in a little deeper. Okay?"

"Well, okay," answered Chum rather crossly. "You have been eating and eating, and I've hardly had any breakfast! Pretty soon it will be too hot to be out in the sun. And you know that there isn't much for me when you go under the trees."

It was plain to see that Chum was feeling very out-of-sorts and was going to be difficult to please. So Pal determined to try to set things straight by working hard to turn over insects— whether he himself ate or not. Consequently, he gave his hoof a real hard kick into the dirt.

"Ouch, ouch—now you did it," hollered Chum. You kicked me—kicked me hard!"

"Oh, I didn't know you were so close to that hoof, Chum. I'm sorry, really sorry. I was trying so hard to turn over more insects."

"I am not going to stay here and be kicked. You need not bother kicking over the dirt again, I'm leaving," pouted the egret. And without a "goodbye" he spread his wings, soared up into the air, and sailed out of sight.

At first Pal was too surprised to feel anything but anger towards Chum. How could his little companion accuse him of deliberately kicking him? How could a friend turn against you as Chum had done?

"Well," thought the little donkey, "I was alone for a long, long time before Chum came and offered to be my friend. And I managed; I can again. I don't need Chum—he doesn't ever have to come back!"

So Pal went on browsing in his pasture. As the day grew hotter, the pesky mosquitoes and flies bit him again and again. He tried to be very brave.

He switched his tail faster and faster. And his ears twitched constantly, but he was miserable!

As the day wore on towards evening the little donkey began to feel his anger fading.

In its place was a feeling of lonesomeness, and although he hated to admit it, he began to realize that he was worried about his little friend. Where was Chum? Was he getting enough to eat? And where would he sleep tonight? "Oh, how I wish Chum would come back," thought Pal. "I think if I tell him how sorry I am that I hurt him—and if I tell him how very much I miss him, maybe he will decide to come back and be my friend again."

The egret was perched on a tree, not far from where the little donkey grazed. He could see Pal, but the leaves kept Pal from seeing him.

He no longer felt angry at Pal because he had had lots of time to think about all that had happened. And he wasn't very proud of himself, either. He remembered how the donkey had said that he was going to try to kick the earth a little harder than he usually did, just to overturn more insects for him. "I should not have been so close to his hoof. I realize that now. He couldn't see me back there. He has always been so gentle—how could I have accused him of kicking me deliberately? I was feeling cross and I took it out on him. After all, I am not bruised, so it was not a hard kick or I'd still feel sore. I don't feel any pain now."

The egret pondered over how he could best make amends so that he and Pal could be good friends again. "What if he doesn't want me? Maybe he doesn't need me at all. I don't provide food for him as he did for me. Oh dear, I wish I hadn't been

21

so disagreeable."

So the donkey stood in his field, wishing his egret friend were back with him keeping him company.

And the egret nested in the tree, prepared to spend a long night feeling badly about the trouble between the two friends. Then he remembered having heard someone—maybe it had been his mother—say, "Never go to sleep without patching up troubles between friends you like."

So getting up courage, just as the moon began to brighten the night, Chum flew over to Pal and perched on the fence where he could watch Pal's face as he offered his apology and asked for Pal to forgive him.

"Pal, I am truly sorry. I was wrong. I miss you, and I hope you will want me back with you again."

"Want you? Oh, yes—please do come stay, Chum. I, too, am sorry that you got hurt. You know I never meant for that to happen."

So, as was their custom, Pal drifted off to sleep, shifting his weight from one hoof to the other. Chum perched in his tree, close to Pal, and he too drifted off to sleep, happy that all was well once more.

Chapter VIII

The Balloons

66 I can't believe my eyes!" exclaimed the little brown donkey. "Look, Chum—look over the barn!"

Chum, the egret, flew up on the gate post to be able to see what Pal was so excited about.

"Oh, the sky is filled with—with? With big birds? Such pretty, colorful birds! But where are their wings?" asked the egret.

"They haven't any wings, Chum. They are round with long skinny tails—like a kite. They are not kites, though. What are they? And where are they coming from? And where are they going?"

"They are going right over our heads, Pal. Look, they seem to be carrying something, too. What do you suppose it is all about?"

As the two friends stood watching the approaching phenomena, they saw all the lovely colors in the drifting objects. Now, as the air currents caught the different objects, some went

23

higher than others. Some traveled faster, too. Pretty soon they were passing by overhead.

"Say, do you suppose those things could be balloons?" asked Chum. "You know, the day I flew to see the circus train—remember? I heard a clown say he had lost some balloons. And another clown said that they'd probably blown away."

"Yes," said the donkey. "I think you are right. Two children walking by yesterday were talking about sending balloons into the sky. I didn't hear when they were going to do it, though. I'll bet that that is where these beautiful balloons are coming from."

"Well, Pal, why don't I just fly over to the school and see if I can find out if we are right. I'd like to know why they would let so many go, too. If I had a balloon, I'd want to hold it tight. I'd never let go!"

"Oh, yes, hurry, Chum. I'll be waiting for you to come back and tell me what is going on."

So the white egret soared up into the air, flew once over the corral to limber up his wings, and then dipped close to the donkey to say, "See you soon," and he was off. He flew carefully in and out between the balloons, being sure that he did not bump any, for he knew his sharp claws or beak could damage the balloons. But he forgot that each balloon was trailing a long piece of string. Suddenly, he felt a tug on his right foot—almost causing him to tip over.

Pal was watching his friend, and he gasped in horror when he saw his little friend seemingly entangled in the string. He brayed loudly, trying to warn Chum to be careful.

"That string will wrap around him so he can't

fly or—," and the donkey shuddered to think that the balloon would float away, taking his friend and he might never see him again.

But as he watched, he saw the egret free himself and again fly between the last few balloons as he went to gather information at the school.

Landing to one side of the playground, out of the way of all the children milling about, excitedly tracking what they each thought was their own balloon, the egret listened to what was being said.

"I bet my balloon will go further than anyone else's," bragged a small boy.

"Oh, no, mine will go further than yours," said another boy. "I can tell."

"How will we know how far they go? asked another child.

"Yes, how will we know? And when will we know? demanded several of the children, as they surrounded their teacher.

"Well," said the teacher, "we are just going to have to wait until the balloons begin to come down. Then we are hoping that they will be seen by someone who will read the note that we attached to each balloon. We hope that whoever reads a note will take the time to let us know. Who remembers what we wrote on the note?"

"I remember," said one of the children. "We put our name, the name of our school, and the telephone number, too."

"Very good, Paul," said the teacher. "But we put something else—anyone remember?"

"We put the address of the school," said Betty.

"Yes," answered the teacher. "Maybe the

balloons will sail so far away that whoever finds them would not want to call on the telephone. That would cost too much. So we asked them to return a post card. That would only cost a few pennies. A telephone call can cost quite a lot."

"Now, does anyone remember what we hoped to learn by having the people tell us about the balloon that they had found?"

One by one, the children offered some of the reasons for the balloon-lift, as it was called.

When the children left to go home, Chum quickly flew back to where Pal was waiting to hear what it was all about.

"What a great idea that was!" exclaimed the donkey. "The balloons looked so pretty!"

"Now, Pal, put on your thinking cap and see if you can tell me what the boys and girls and the teachers, too, hoped to learn from their experiment. Do you know?"

The little donkey tried very hard, but all he could suggest was that the children wanted to see all the bright colors.

"No," said Chum, "there were many more important things that they hoped to learn."

"Like what?" asked Pal.

"Like learning how far the farthest balloon might go," answered Chum, quite pleased with himself. "And how close by one might come down, too."

"I wish one had landed here in our corral," said Pal, wistfully. "But I guess we couldn't have answered the note, so it is just as well."

"The notes asked people to tell where they found the balloon, and at what time, too," added

Chum. "That would tell the children something about the speed and the direction of the wind."

"There were other science facts that could be learned," said Pal. "I can undertand that."

"Best of all, though, the children would be meeting new people, learning about where they live and about their lives," said Chum.

The two friends enjoyed talking about the balloon-lift for days and days. When the children passed by on their way to and from school, the donkey and the egret listened eagerly for any news they might hear as to how many post cards were returned to school.

How they wished that they could be students—learning about the world was such fun!

Chapter IX

The Rustlers!

There was no moon that night—no moon and no stars. The sky was covered with black, rain-laden clouds that scudded over the fields and pastures. The wind had an eerie sound as it, too, swept across the fields. It was a spooky night.

The little brown donkey was sleeping on his feet, as he 'most always did. At least, there were no mosquitoes bothering him, thanks to the wind. His friend, the egret, was up in a tree which grew just outside the corral. He was sleeping despite the swaying of the branches.

Suddenly a noise woke the donkey. He twitched his long ears this way and that, trying to determine from what direction the noise was coming.

But all was quiet again and he decided that he must have had a bad dream. Just as he was almost asleep again, the noise reached his ears a second time. Something about that noise seemed

28

to say "Danger!"

By now, the donkey had pinpointed the direction of the sound. It was coming from the pasture where the cows were kept.

"Clip, clip, clip,"—a wire was being cut. Then a truck motor started up and there were low voices—men's voices.

Suddenly, a cow began to moo loudly, and she woke up the other cows, who took up the call, all bawling at once. It wasn't long until the voices were yelling, adding to the din, as the men tried to quiet the cows.

The egret flew down to be beside his friend. They were both afraid because they had never heard either a truck or men in the cow pasture so late at night. What was going on?

A light came on in the farmhouse, and two men with powerful flashlights went running towards the cow pasture.

As the two friends, Pal and Chum, listened, they heard a shout.

"Let's get out of here! Now!" yelled a voice. The truck roared down the lane heading for the road just as the two men from the farmhouse reached the pasture. Their cow dog ran ahead of them, growling and sniffing about the lane and the hole in the fence that showed up in the flashlight's beam.

"Well, would you look at that!" hollered the farmer to his son. "Rustlers—I can't believe it. Rustlers! Did they get any of our cattle?"

"No, Dad," answered his son. "They all seem to be accounted for as near as I can see with my flashlight."

The cows were quiet now. They knew the farmer and his son, and they felt quite secure with them there.

"Dad, you go back to the house and call the sheriff's department," suggested the son. "I'll look for anything that might help us learn who those rustlers are."

"Wow!" said Pal. "Did you hear that, Chum? Rustlers! Rustlers in our field. I'm glad the cows frightened them away with all their bawling, aren't you, Chum?"

Chum agreed. He hadn't realized until it was all over how frightened he had been. Not for himself, because he could have flown quickly away from his perch in the tree. No, he was concerned that some harm might come to his dear friend, Pal. He was ready, despite his fear, to try to defend Pal. "I could peck at someone with my sharp beak—or flutter my wings in their faces if I had to," he thought.

Well, the excitement wasn't over even then, because pretty soon the wail of the police siren was heard, drawing nearer and nearer. The patrol car, with its large sheriff's emblem, turned in the lane. As it approached the hole that the rustlers had made in the fence, the sheriff's deputy turned on a powerful spotlight on the side of his car, lighting up the field as though it were daylight. He stopped the car, making sure that he kept to one side, as he had coming up the lane. He didn't want to cover the tire marks made by the truck.

After reporting his location to headquarters over the walkie-talkie, he got out and joined the farmer's son, who told him why he had been called.

"Rustlers again!" exclaimed the deputy. "They are keeping us busy these dark, moonless nights. But we'll get them yet. They will get careless and do something that will make it possible for us to learn their identity."

The officer studied the tracks that the truck's tires had left on the ground. By measuring them with a special instrument, he could tell that it hadn't been a very heavy truck, although it certainly had to be big enough to carry at least one cow if the rustlers had been successful in their raid.

Chum and Pal were very interested in what was happening. Now, the clouds had gone and the sun was a big orange ball in the east.

"I'll fly over there, Pal, and see if I can find out just what is going on. Then I'll come back and tell you all about it while we eat our breakfast."

"Good, I wish you would, Chum," said Pal. "You always bring back such interesting stories. It's almost as good as my being there—almost."

A little while later, after the patrol car had gone and after the farmer and his son had repaired the fence, Chum returned.

Pal had Chum's breakfast all ready for him—all those juicy, tasty bugs. And when last seen, they were busily going over all the details of that exciting night—the night they almost seemed to be on a western frontier.

Chapter X

The Rains Come
Spring Is Here

D ay after day the sun had been shining. The fields were dry; the ditches held no water. The grass was no longer green, but a dull brown. The little brown donkey had to graze on the outside of the fence now, as there was not much for him to eat inside his corral. It hurt his neck as he stretched it between the barbed wires to reach for a bit of green grass here and there. The egret seemed to find plenty of insects still, as Pal stirred up the dry soil. But neither of them had much pep—the days were too hot, the fields too barren.

Then one dusty hot afternoon, as the donkey and his friend, the egret, took shelter under a tree, hiding from the sun, they heard a low rumble in the sky. Way off in the distance, but coming in their direction, was a formation of large, black, angry-looking clouds. The wind blew up in sharp gusts, sending dust swirling over the fields. And then a few drops of water followed, slowly at first but soon coming down in a heavy torrent of rain. There was thunder, and lightning flashed as the storm mounted in fury.

Pal and Chum, instinctively knowing that it was dangerous to be under a tree during a thunderstorm, moved out into the corral and let the rain cool their warm bodies. It felt *so* good!

"Guess the drought is over, Chum," observed Pal. "We need rain *so* badly. My water bucket was almost dry. Listen to the splash of raindrops in it now."

"Yes, and look, Pal. The rain has caused some juicy worms to come up out of the ground. I like that!" answered Chum.

When the storm had passed by, traveling north over the river, Chum and Pal wandered around their yard enjoying the new fragrance in the air.

"I feel restless, Pal," said Chum. "I have a funny feeling—something makes me feel as though I'm being tugged to fly somewhere, but I don't know where. Do you feel that way too?"

"No," said Pal. "I have a feeling, though, that there is a real change in the air. I feel sort of lonesome, and yet I'm not really lonesome with you here, my friend."

"That is exactly how I feel, too," said Chum. "A lonesome feeling—but something else, too."

That night both the donkey and the egret slept fitfully. There seemed to be a mysterious something hovering over them. What could it be?

The following day, towards late afternoon, the black clouds began to billow and build up, making an angry-looking sky, as they had the day before.

"Look, Chum, it's going to rain again," called Pal. "Bet we will have rain every day for awhile."

"You are right," agreed Chum. "This must be close to our rainy season. Each Spring is like this, remember? Winter must be over now."

"I feel restless today—just as you did yesterday, Chum. Do you feel restless again today?"

"Oh, yes, I certainly do! What do you suppose is the matter with us?"

"It will go away—this funny yearning feeling, I think," said Pal. "We'll have more to eat now that the grass is growing again and turning green, you'll see."

Just as they had predicted, the rains did come, day after day. The trees had more leaves, the grass was greener, and bees began to buzz from flower to flower, drinking the nectar in the blossoms.

"Pal, would you mind if I took a little flight? I want to see where all the other egrets are flying to each evening. Did you notice that they do not stay with the cows as they did before the rain?"

"No," admitted Pal. "I haven't noticed. But look—you are right. They are flying out of sight over the hill right now!"

Before Pal had finished talking, Chum rose in the air and took off after the other egrets. He dipped once over Pal—his way of saying "I'll be back!" Then he spread his wings and off he went until he was just a speck in the distance.

Pal felt quite deserted. He had seen how restless Chum had been the last few weeks, and he felt that maybe he would be losing his dear friend.

That night he listened eagerly for the sound of Chum's return. But Chum did not come back. Nor did he come the next night. Pal missed Chum, and kept a watchful eye, scanning the skies to see if he would spot Chum returning.

One day, as Pal grazed in his corral, he finally heard the whir of wings. He looked up and saw Chum returning at last. But Chum wasn't alone. He flew down beside Pal, while a lovely white girl egret settled down beside him.

"Hi, Pal! I want you to meet my mate. Isn't she lovely? I call her 'Honey.' She and I have built a nest high in a tree on a little island not too far from here. Lots of egrets have nests there too. And before long there will be baby egrets. I am so happy, Pal. We will all come to visit you each day. Then you will have lots of friends. And I can still explore for you. But now, we'll have lots of eyes to see the sights— and neither of us need feel restless any more."

"That's nice for you," said Pal sadly. "But, Chum, you will be with Honey now. And I just have to learn to accept that. I do love having you here. You know that. Come whenever you want—I'll always be glad to see you."

In his heart, Pal knew that things would never be the same again. He would just have to make the best of it. Liking Chum as he did, he was glad that Chum had found a mate—he wanted Chum to be happy.

So, he passed his days in the corral, always watching and listening for Chum's visits. He found himself feeling very restless and lonely. "I wonder if I'll ever find a new friend," he thought. Or—and this was such a new idea he couldn't quite grasp it—"I wonder if, someday, I'll have a mate, too. That would be just too wonderful!"

Chapter XI

The Auction

The farmer in whose field Pal and Chum had spent so much time together was watching the little brown donkey from his kitchen window.

"Mother," he called to his wife who was bustling around getting the supper on the table. "Come see the little brown donkey. He doesn't look as well as he had all winter. Sometimes his oats have hardly been touched. He stands with his head down, as he used to do before—" the farmer went on, "—before that little white egret settled in the corral with him."

"Yes, I noticed how sad he seems again, dear. The egret comes still, but doesn't stay. And he has a mate with him now. I think that they have a nest and will be having a family soon," said the farmer's wife.

The farmer was a kindly man. He cared for his animals. He made sure they had food and a constant supply of water. But he had never really been concerned about their being happy. Now he felt badly for the little brown donkey. He wondered what he could do to help him.

His wife felt as he did. She had so often enjoyed watching the two friends together. She had observed how the egret would fly off to investigate anything unusual that took place. She saw the egret come back each time and saw the two close together. She did not realize, though, that the egret related all he had seen to the donkey.

"Well, dear," she said. "I am sure we can't find another egret for him. Maybe another will come as that one had done. Suppose we go to the library and look up a book about egrets? If we knew what they liked to eat, perhaps we could place some egret food out in the corral to attract another egret."

"Dear, the egrets like all the bugs that are disturbed by the cows' or the donkey's feet. They don't need grain or seeds, so I don't think your plan will work."

A few weeks went by. The donkey did not seem to want his food very much, and he began to get quite thin and listless.

"Oh, dear me, we have got to do something for him," said the farmer. "I just can't bear to watch him any more. But what can we do?"

The next day the farmer went to an auction in hopes of finding a nice horse or pony for his daughter. His wife loved horses too, so she went along.

Such beautiful horses were on sale. There were American-bred, Appaloosas, Pintos, Tennessee Walkers, as well as the great Clydesdales with their

Ann Gedney

beautiful feathered feet. Some Arabian horses were there too. Such beautiful animals!

While the farmer was busy looking over the saddle horses, his wife wandered down to the pens where quite a few animals, not for sale, were kept. Some of them had just come by train from out west. They would have to be trained to be safe and obedient for people to ride before they could be sold. This is what the cowboys did—trained them to accept a bridle and a saddle. And they taught them how to respond to the reins.

All of a sudden the farmer's wife—her name was Sandra—heard a sound different from the sounds that horses make. She listened. There it was again! It seemed to be coming from the last pen. It was a rather harsh sound, although not a loud one. What could be making such a noise? Just then she remembered having heard a sound just like it, only much, much louder, back on the farm.

"Why, it must be a donkey," she thought. "It sounds like our donkey. I must go see if I am right."

She hurried to the last pen, looked over the top of the gate, and sure enough, there was a lovely little brown donkey with the prettiest brown eyes! It was love at first sight. Sandra stretched out her hand with one of the carrots she had put in her pocket to give to the horse they were buying. The donkey gently ate the treat off her outstretched hand and pawed the ground as though she was saying "thank you."

"You dear little donkey," Sandra said. "I wish I could take you home. Why, that's it!" she continued, talking to herself now. "That's what we'll do. We'll take you home to keep our little brown donkey happy. I'm sure he'd love having you with him!"

She hurried off to find her husband and see if he would agree to such a plan. As she went through the crowds, she remembered that the horses in those pens were not for sale. Perhaps the donkey was not for sale either. "Oh, dear, I do hope it can be bought," she thought. "And I hope my husband will agree to buy it, if it is for sale. I have a birthday coming soon, and this donkey will be my present. And our little brown donkey's present, too." Sandra didn't know that her donkey had been named 'Pal' by his egret friend.

She finally found her husband, who was patting a beautiful Pinto pony. When he saw Sandra he said, "What do you think of this Pinto for Sharon, Sandra? Isn't it a beauty? And it's only three years old, just right to train for riding the trails."

"Yes, dear, it's a beautiful Pinto. I know Sharon will be so delighted. She is a lucky little girl! But, dear, I've found one I very much would like for my birthday. Do come see. It is down at the end of the stables in a pen. I just love it. I know you will too."

So they hurried off to see Sandra's find. "Why do you want a saddle horse, dear? You never ride any more," asked the farmer.

When they reached that last pen and the farmer, whose name was Steve, looked in, he began to laugh. "Honey, you can't ride that little jenny. She is much too small!"

"Oh, I don't want to ride the donkey. I want it as a friend for our own little sad fellow," exclaimed Sandra. Then she thought a minute.

"You called it 'Jenny.' Did you know it was here? Have you seen it before? How did you know its—I mean—her name, Steve?" she demanded.

"Now wait a minute, Sandra. I've never seen this jenny before. 'Jenny' is what a *girl donkey* is called, dear," he explained.

"Oh, a girl donkey," Sandra said. "I bet our donkey—he *is* a boy donkey, isn't he?—would love having a jenny for a mate. Then he wouldn't be so lonesome ever again. Please go see if 'Jenny' is for sale, dear."

Steve hurried off to find the owner of the stable.

"Well, Steve," the owner said, "that little jenny is not to be auctioned. I was just looking for a good home for her since my children, whose pet she is, are now away at school. I know how well you and Sandra take care of your animals. Do take her, and I hope you will all enjoy her as much as my family has. She is lonesome with the children no longer around to pet her."

So Jenny was put in the horse trailer alongside of the new Pinto, and they all headed for home. Pal would soon have a mate to share his corral.

Won't he be surprised!

Chapter XII

Pal and Jenny

As the farmer and his wife drove into the driveway in their station wagon with the horse van trailing behind them, the new saddle horse whinnied softly. He had gotten the scent of the other horses stabled nearby. And the little jenny stamped her small hooves, impatient to be led out of the van and into her new home. It had been a long tiring ride trying to keep her balance as the van swayed behind the car for so many miles since they had left the auction for their new home.

Over in the corral the small donkey stirred in his sleep. The noises of the animals at the stable began to rouse him. He listened, trying to make out what was going on so late at night. "Oh, how I miss Chum," he thought. "If he were still here he would have gone to see what was happening at the stable. And then he would have come back and told me all about it." Pal twitched his long ears—first one way, then another—straining to recognize the voices and the low whinny of the horses as they welcomed the new arrivals.

Suddenly something else got Pal's attention. Something he didn't hear—didn't see—but which he could sense with his nostrils. Something that made him tingle with excitement, although he could not tell why. Now he was wide awake and more curious than ever.

Pal listened for quite a long time. But, after the barn door was closed—he did recognize that sound—and the lights in the house went off, Pal could hear no more sounds. Nor was that mysterious scent still tickling his imagination. So, he settled down to sleep once more. Try as he did, sleep would not come. What was it in the air that kept Pal too keyed up to sleep?

As morning came and the sun chased the stars away, Chum flew over the fence for his daily visit with Pal.

"Am I glad to see you!" exclaimed Pal. "How I wished you were here last night!"

"Why, what's up?" Chum asked. "Last night didn't seem different than any other night. Not to me, anyway. I suppose it is lonely for you, Pal. I'm sorry I can't be here with you as I used to be. But, as you know, I am busy raising a family now, so I must stay near the nest."

"Yes, I know. And it's okay, Chum. It's just that I miss you and all the exciting stories you used to tell me. Last night I hardly slept at all. When I hear noises I become very curious."

"Where were the noises coming from, Pal?" asked the egret. "What were they like? Do you still hear them? If you do, I'll go now and find out what

43

is happening."

"No, I do not hear anything right now," replied the donkey. "It is still very early. No one seems to be outside over at the barn."

"I'll bet that the noises were coming from the stable, Pal," said Chum.

"You are right. That is just where all the activity was late last night. But you surely couldn't see or hear it from your nesting tree. How do you know?"

"I didn't see nor hear it. But I did see the station wagon go by pulling the double horse van quite late last night," answered Chum.

"That is what it was, I am sure," said Pal. "I remember hearing the horses whinny and I heard the barn door being closed. Then the lights went off in the house. Sh-sh, I just hear the door being opened now. I forgot to tell you the strangest part, Chum. There was a scent in the air—one I'd never gotten before. It seemed to make me feel tingly and excited—but why, I have no idea. Quick, Chum! Do go over and see what is going on. I've just got to know!"

As the egret settled himself on a gate post near the stable, he watched the farmer lead a beautiful new saddle pony out into the yard. The farmer brushed the pony until its coat was glossy. Then he put a new saddle and bridle on it and led it around the yard a few times before calling his daughter.

"Sharon, please come out here," he called. "I need you."

"I'm coming, Daddy," a voice inside the house answered. "I'll be right there."

The door opened and Sharon came running down the steps and through the yard. As she rounded the corner, she stopped, wide-eyed, as she saw the beautiful horse that her daddy was holding by the bridle.

"Oh, Daddy, what a beautiful, beautiful horse! May I ride him—please, please? And what a handsome leather saddle and bridle!"

"Yes, dear, you may. And happy birthday from mother and me," he added, as he put his arm around Mrs. Perkins, who had followed Sharon out to the stable to join in the excitement of seeing Sharon when she realized that the horse was hers.

"Ride him, honey. Be careful, for he doesn't know his new home as yet. We bought him at the auction last night so that we could surprise you. He is yours to name and to care for each day," added Mrs. Perkins. "Happy birthday, dear!"

Sharon mounted the pony, after giving her parents a big kiss and said "Thank you, Mom and Dad," as she rode off through the field.

Just as Chum was getting ready to fly back to Pal to relate all he had seen, he heard a donkey's bray. Surprised, he listened again. No, it wasn't coming from Pal's corral. It seemed to be coming from inside the stable. So he stayed on the gate post trying to solve the mystery before returning to Pal.

Mr. and Mrs. Perkins looked at each other as they went into the stable. They seemed to be sharing a secret. A secret that made them quite happy.

A few minutes later they returned, leading a beautiful small donkey that looked almost like Pal,

45

although a bit smaller. Chum couldn't believe his eyes.

"Shall we introduce Jenny to our little friend over in his corral? He is going to be even more surprised than Sharon was with her birthday gift."

Well, Chum didn't want to spoil the surprise by telling Pal ahead of time. So he took his time getting back, but made sure he was there to see when Pal first saw the jenny.

Pal was eagerly watching the sky for Chum's return and he didn't notice Mr. and Mrs. Perkins as they approached his gate. But that tantalizing scent was growing stronger and stronger. Pal quivered with excitement.

Just as Chum settled on a gate post in the farthest corner of Pal's corral, Mr. and Mrs. Perkins opened the gate. Pal heard the catch click and he turned eagerly to receive whatever treat was in store for him—perhaps an apple, a carrot, or a ration of oats. He stopped abruptly and looked in disbelief at the little jenny being let into the corral with him. Then, remembering his manners, he went up to the jenny, nuzzling her softly in greeting. She returned his greeting and trotted around to stand at his side.

"Oh, honey, see! They like each other already!" exclaimed Mrs. Perkins to her husband. Then she patted Pal and said, "Little donkey, we've brought you a jenny so you will no longer be lonely. You must be good to her and share your corral and the food and water, too." She gave them each a small apple and then she and Mr. Perkins walked out, closing the gate as they went. They walked arm-in-arm back to the house, delighted with all the pleasure their two surprises had given—one to their daughter and one to the little donkey.

Pal saw his friend on the gate post and he trotted over to share his excitement and to introduce the jenny to his best friend, his only friend, really, up to now.

"Oh, Pal, I'm so happy for you. You will never be all alone again. I shall still come, maybe with my family, and we will share all our good times as we have in the past." said Chum.

As he flew off back to his mate on their nest, he saw Pal and Jenny strolling happily around the corral, getting to know each other.

And, who knows? Maybe someday they'll be raising a family, too.

The End

AUTHOR BIOGRAPHY

Kathleen Cail Dahlquist was born in Boston, Massachusetts. She graduated from Leslie College, Cambridge, Massachusetts and William Paterson College, Wayne, New Jersey, with a Bachelor's Degree and Masters in Education.

She was a director of several nursery schools in Massachusetts and New Jersey. She was a kindergarten teacher in Oakland, New Jersey from 1966 to 1981.

Kathleen retired to Venice, Florida in the early 1980s. Her story is based on her retirement location.

She was active in volunteer work as a Gray Lady in Ridgewood, New Jersey. In Venice, Florida, Kathleen did volunteer work as a member of HAV of Venice Hospital as well as for the Red Cross. She has volunteered for Garden Grove School and Venice Elementary, working with the kindergarten classes.

Kathleen's hobbies include tennis, horseback riding, swimming, shuffleboard, writing poetry and children's stories and dancing, both line dancing and ballroom.